THE BLUES AND BROWNS OF THE TWIN LANDS OF KIARALOT AND DONEKIARATALL

Dr. Damaris-Lois Yamoah Lang

[Dr. D-L Y Lang]

Illustrated by: Lika Kvirikashvili

Editor: Dr. Enid Stubin

The Blues and Browns of the twin lands of Kiaralot and Donekiaratall
"The love of hate changes the diversity of our unique differences into prejudices that stir up harmful actions, consciously or subconsciously"
"If showing your worth requires you to ascribe worthlessness to another, then you are the worthless one"

ISBN: 978-1-7378950-0-8 (Paperback)
ISBN: 978-1-7378950-1-5 (ebook)

Library of Congress Control Number: 2021918531

Any references to historical events, real people, or real places are used fictitiously. Names, characters, and places are products of the author's imagination.

Printed in the United States of America

DEDICATION TO

Milo F.Z. Lang

Contents

Preface

"Juneteenth," celebrating the date of the emancipation of the last slaves in the United States of America, also marks the first meeting of an Education-Advocacy group, P-CoC Inc | Parenting Children of Color, on June 19th, 2020, at the residence of Dr. Damaris-Lois Yamoah Lang, the Founder, and President. Dr. Lang, whose doctoral work focused on the neurobiology of behavior (paternal care), explains that social behaviors, including racism and colorism, stem from the brain's perceptions. She emphasized that addressing racial inequities in our society will require curtailing negative outside influx, which causes a shift in our facial and skin-tone recognition brain, primed for survival instinct, from entering the realm of unconscious bias expressed as racial stereotypes. In a relatively straightforward story, the author scales down the complexity of the underlying mechanisms shaping our socio-structural interactions into a simple account to reflect the gist of society's discriminatory practices fueled by stereotypes that lead to prejudices and biases against the marginalized.

Introduction

Being humane as a human is the essence of being a Human Being, and freedom is the bedrock of experiencing the heart of humanity. However, freedom without liberation is still bondage—the current state of our world is in disrepair, and we cannot continue to give it the blind eye. Although it is a common understanding that ignorance is bliss and knowledge is power, we must wisely choose our areas of ignorance and knowledge.

A vivid danger is imminent when falsehood overpowers truth and incoherently stated facts become manipulated to create misrepresentations as alternate truths. Thus, education is critical in providing the knowledge and understanding to equip decision-making processes that solely seek a solution-oriented approach that serves all. However, such informed engagements must utilize a bedrock of goodwill, preventing problem-solving from becoming problem-creating.

The health of our future depends on current and past diagnoses. The practicality of this work heavily lies in the investment we provide now and not later to our children—our future. Because if adulthood brought with it sensibility, our world-ruled by adults would not be in its current disarray. From a newly born child to the oldest person alive today, every living human has up to a maximum of 100 summers to help fix our world. Albeit, based on the average population of our world, around 75% of the population will have up to only 50 summers to make a significant impact to improve our world. Thus, 25% of our current population—our children in their formative years (up to 20years)—will require us, adults, to provide adequate support that prepares them to create a world of equitable co-existence for all.

The revamping of an equal and equitable education focuses on a responsive approach for all people, not only in the sense of culture but also, more importantly, those who by birth assume genetically diverse traits, such as our IEP students and the racially marginalized.

The first step to progress is identifying the unlevel pathways short of providing a socially healthy and equitable society through our schools and communities. Chimamanda Ngozi Adichie stated that "the single-story creates stereotypes. The problem with stereotypes is not that they are untrue but that they are incomplete. They make one story become the only story..."

This tale of two towns presents us with a history that has plagued the current state of the societies enforced by stereotypes and how one simple mindset catalyzed a dichotomous direction between the two neighboring towns.

Chapter 1

We love Kiaralot

How does it feel to know you live in the best country in the world? According to research conducted by the United Worlds, Kiaralot has been consistently named the best country to live in and raise a family. The research considered factors such as care for all citizens in the areas of health, education, equitable wage, economy, low crime rates, social health of all communities, including those with ethnic diversity, and life expectancy rates.

"Hello everyone, I am Ynlad, and this is my brother Gnalolim; he is my blood brother.

Ynlad

Gnalolim

We are mixed-race kids. Wait, let me correct that.   We are part of the human race with mixed ethnicities. Gnalolim and I appear quite different from each other because the set of genes producing the phenotypic expression of hair color and skin color are co-dominant and linked to the X chromosomes . . . Uhm, well, in simple terms, we look different because of how our genes work.

Our parents are the most amazing human beings we've ever known. Our dad is a philosopher and jazz musician from the Blue ethnic group. Our mom, Dlyl, is a policy manager and social activist from the Brown ethnic group in Donekiaratall. We grew up mostly in Kiaralot, but our parents visited Donekiaratall often. Gnalolim is a physician-scientist with an MD and a Ph.D. in Oncology and Neuroscience, respectively. He loves the outdoors and enjoys skiing and skating. I am a geneticist, and for fun, I like to read and travel the world.

You may be wondering what makes Kiaralot the best country in the world. Anigroeg, a renowned historian, explained that Kiaralot was not always a paradise. Most people entertained the erroneous assumption that Kiaralot maintained its best-country status by promoting itself as a land endowed with rich resources and people with high intelligence. But one factor accounted for Kiaralot's success as a land: its people of elaborate ethnic diversity were able to co-exist in harmony, enjoying the goodness of life.

Here is a story that will illustrate what set Kiaralot apart through a shared history with the people of its twin land, Donekiaratall.

Trigger to dig deep

Teragram, our dad's great-great-grandmother, shared her story about living and growing up in Kiaralot. She said that more often than not, she felt as though she did not belong. This was the result of the treatment she received in her community and at school. Her schoolmates treated her as if she were not important, as if they were better than she was. One day in class, the teacher was discussing a topic with her students when she posed a question that required critical thinking skills. Teragram looked around and then raised her hand, as no one else had put a hand up. The teacher glanced at Teragram and turned away, apparently in search of another raised hand. Another student, Leztruw, raised his hand, and the teacher called on him. Leztruw answered incorrectly. Teragram put her hand up, but the teacher refused to acknowledge her. She could hear her classmates whispering, "She doesn't know anything. *Whores* are dumb." Teragram was familiar with the word *whores*. It was a name people used to describe individuals with wavy yellow hair with a blue tinge like Teragram's – a distinct feature of all Blues. This was not the first time Teragram had heard herself called that, and hearing her classmates' murmuring those words made her feel diminished. Teragam stated that she vividly remembers her teacher glaring at her irritatedly and then saying, "Teragram, are you sure you can answer this question? It is pretty intellectually tasking, and you wouldn't want to look foolish, would you?" Teragram slowly lowered her hand while muttering the answer to herself. The teacher then provided the answer to the class. She was about to move on when Knarf, a non-Blue student, spoke up: " I heard Teragram. She gave the correct answer." The teacher, Ronaele, slowly turned to Teragram and made a condescending, applauding gesture: "Huh! Interestingly impressive. You certainly must be an exception."

Gnalolim and I listened to our great-great-grandmother's story with utter disgust. We felt the poisonous fear of worthlessness engulf Teragram all over again as she spoke. We were beside ourselves at how this magnitude of psychological cruelty could be placed on a child in any land, let alone Kiaralot, the utopia of the world?

The day we heard this story is when Gnalolim and I, together with colleagues, decided to embark on a journey: we would study and do research to learn how a toxic place could turn into the most enlightened place in the world? Our findings would lead us to the discovery and understanding of the stories of ethnic lineages once considered the bottom rung of society in the land of Kiaralot and Donekiaratall.

Our adventure reveals the respective stories of hope--and hope deferred-- for the Blue and Brown people of the twin lands of Kiaralot and Donekiaratall.

Blues of Kiaralot

Browns of Donekiaratall

Chapter

2

Birthing the lie

The histories of the Blues and Browns are remarkably similar. The Blues of the land of Kiaralot was so named because of the blue highlights in their yellow hair. The Browns lived in Donekiaratall and were called so because their melanin appears uniformly on their skin, unlike the group known as the Pinks, whose melanin is distributed on their skin surface as freckled black or brown dots.

"whores"
(human-coital tools)

"niggers"
(human-work tools)

The Blues and Browns were both enslaved in the past, forced into work with no recourse. The Blues were given the derogatory name of "whores" to signify their forced service into sexual slavery and as society's surrogates - human bearers for the "elite" wives of other ethnic groups who somehow did not want to endure the pains and stress of childbirth.

The Browns were called "niggers," representing their existence as dominated workers at the service of other ethnic groups in the land of Donekiaratall. The terms "whores" and "niggers" are ingrained in the society's fabric as respective symbols of a human-coital tool and a human-work tool, commodities at the disposal of other humans.

Dr. Haomay, a respected historian and a cognitive neuropsychologist, explained that in the past, the Blues of Kiaralot, by dint of their anatomical features, were considered intellectually inferior. In Donekiaratall, individuals with uniformly tanned skin tones, the Browns, were considered inferior to pale-skin-toned people. This mindset was not attributed to one particular ethnicity but became widespread and created a social caste system based entirely on skin tones.

What took over was the use of hate in reducing diversity and individuality into prejudices that stirred up harmful behavior, whether consciously or subconsciously. Dr. Haomay explained that the propagated belief attributed to Blues and Browns took root with the creation of what he called the "Camouflage Mental Creep" – a mastering craft of manipulating people's thinking to align with a harmful ideology. This, he stated, is a most dangerous assertion of human power.

As history revealed, this led to acts of barbaric, horrific, inhumane violence against the Blues and Browns. The masterminds behind the viciousness were known as the "Pale-faces" or "Pales," so named for their extremely light skin tones. Like the Browns, the Pales did not come from a single ethnic group but several others.

The Pales imputed dehumanizing ideologies on the Blues and Browns in their separate lands. They committed atrocious acts of human trafficking, rape, brutality, murder, and enslavement on the people, impacting both lands.

In Kiaralot, the Pales propagated the dehumanization of the Blues in relation to all other ethnic groups, including the Browns. While in Donekiaratall the Pales committed the same acts against all Browns related to other ethnic groups in that land, including Blue individuals. Of course, the separate impact of the Pales' systematic oppression was maintained because the events pre-dated the rise of technology and globalization. The fundamental predicament of the Blues and Browns in their separate lands was that they weren't allowed to present themselves alongside any other ethnic group unless it was with an air of inferiority.

Ecarg, our dad's great-great-aunt, a Blue, recollected that her grandparents were severely punished when they were found attempting to educate themselves. Her grandmother was whipped with barbed wire that tore up her skin, left outside amidst flies circling her bloody, naked body when she was left outside without food for 24 hours, only because she had said something that reflected her natural intelligence. In the process, she inadvertently appeared to shame a non-Blue. These extreme measures against Blues pressured many of them to play dumb to avoid persecution and retaliation.

Harmful ideologies resemble swarms of mosquitoes, seemingly innocuous but capable of spreading life-threatening diseases. As a result, generations down the line, the status quo lends itself to making pale-skinned individuals benefit socially and economically from exploiting the Blues of Kiaralot and the Browns of Donekiaratall.

Fight or Flight

The physical features distinguishing the Blues and the Browns are impossible to conceal. These individuals are easily picked out of a crowd. Historians learned that most Blues and Browns tried ways to escape to other lands. At that time, very few succeeded.

Browns in Freedom Cities

Blues in Freedom Cities

However, all was not lost. In the land of Donekiaratall, a Brown named Egernaob began to mobilize individuals, referred to as the "holistic freedom-fighters," to fight against the oppression they faced. Word of Egernaob's courage and advocacy quickly spread into the land of Kiaralot. The holistic freedom- fighters in both lands focused on two main things: freedom for Blues and Browns from enslavement and freedom for everyone from ideologies ingrained in the society as dehumanizing stereotypes.

Holistic Freedom-Fighters of Kiaralot

Holistic Freedom-Fighters of Donekiaratall

Freedom from enslavement during years of grueling combat was relatively easier to achieve than obtaining freedom for all from dehumanizing ideologies against

Blues and Browns. In the land of Donekiaratall, achieving the Browns' freedom has been close to impossible, while in Kiaralot, the process, though difficult, was relatively simple to accomplish.

In pursuit of holistic freedom for everyone, some challenges significantly extended the timeline for achieving equity for the people of Kiaralot. These challenges were solution-oriented initiatives that were agathokakological or composed of what we might call both positive and negative aspects, according to Dr. Haomay. The hit-and-miss effect of these intended solutions was used as evidence in debates submerged in biased standpoints. One such example was that most assumed that following freedom from enslavement, the extension of courteous or "nice" treatment of the Blues and Browns was in itself sufficient to allow equitable co-existence. This is far from the truth. Freedom from enslavement is one step, but how does "niceness" or "courtesy" eliminate harmful and negative stereotypes woven into the fabric of society?

Chapter 3

Understanding the scope of the problem

Gnalolim and his peers had researched the concept of relatedness to establish an active approach to "unlearning" harmful stereotypes that have plagued certain social cultures. Relatedness in connecting abstract concepts to tangible ones is an important way to foster learning. He explained that our brains naturally resort to relatedness in assessing a novel environment. Relatedness is useful in both active and passive learning practices. Relatedness practices help to define or explain concepts by connecting them to familiar ones. For example, we recognize the following images through their functions: red light to mean stop, the green light to mean go; military uniforms; doctor's white coat. However, this same strategy of relatedness can be used to create harm. An example: Relatedness is used to recognize the ideology of whiteness as good and superior over blackness, which is often deemed bad and inferior. This seemingly irrelevant concept has seeped into associations made between skin tones and skin color as expressed in individuals of white and black cultures. This ideology occurs across all ethnicities as expressed in societal norms, media, and--most treacherously--educational institutions. The birth and acceptance of stereotypes are harmful to the very existence of others.

Together with other allies, our family has pioneered fighting for freedom from dehumanizing and harmful stereotypes in the lands of Donekiaratall and Kiaralot. The work we've done has remained effective and productive, largely because it relies heavily on civic engagement with society through communities and schools.

Initiating the second part of the twofold holistic freedom for the Blues and Browns required the unlearning of concepts that generate biases and the removal of norms that perpetuate harmful stereotypes against the Blues and Browns. These processes were far from being recognized. The undoing of such psychological damage ingrained in the society's fabric will certainly be an arduous task to accomplish.

Typical Donekiaratall classroom

Typical Kiaralot classroom

The holistic freedom fighters resorted to community members and expert advice to commence work towards achieving the second goal of holistic freedom. Our mom, Dlyl, and her colleagues mobilized members of the community who had diverse backgrounds, ranging from scientists, stay-home parents, teachers, janitors, elders, children--anyone who was willing to know, understand,

and learn the strategies--to practice this solution-oriented process.

The initial step was facing the problem by clearly stating the underlining factors of ethnic inequity. The next step was to strategize ways to provide workable solutions. Finally, the work would determine practical ways to implement the strategic suggestions.

Time to Unearth and Unravel

The first step necessary is to identify the factors causing the issues, understanding the impact the issues create and defining these issues to deal with the problem. The holistic freedom team identified some important elements.

First, the history of the Blues and Browns did not consist of their own narratives. The school curricula were filled with the work of authors who were non-Blue and non-Brown. The content of the books was not those of the victims but rather the perspectives of observers and sometimes oppressors. This approach led to blind spots and a far-from-authentic portrayal of the whole narrative of the Blues and Browns.

Non-Brown Narrator in Donekiaratall

Non-Blue Narrator in Kiaralot

Second, the Blues and Browns had no input in the curriculum design. Children of the Blues and Browns had no space to learn about themselves and their norms, lifestyles, and cultures. The only information they had was the horrors of their past in history books and literature. There was no mention of the strides they had made in society and the massive contributions and innovations they made and continue to make in diverse fields and careers, such as architecture, science, and mathematics.

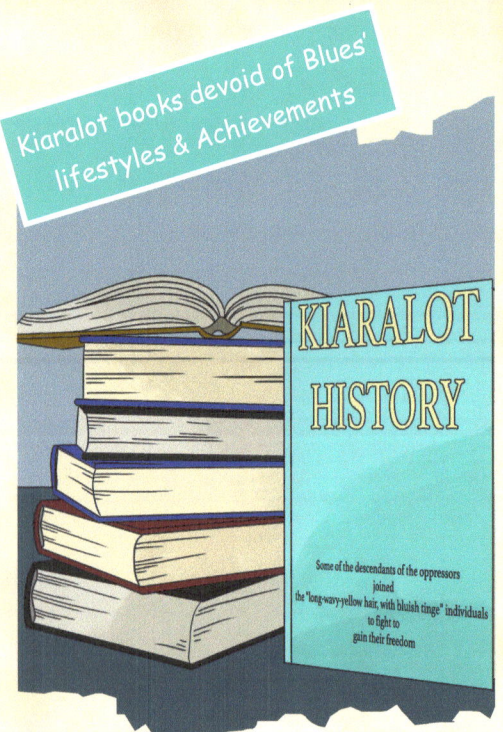

Kiaralot books devoid of Blues' lifestyles & Achievements

Donekiaratall books devoid of Browns' lifestyles & Achievements

Third, most teachers were not adequately trained in the pedagogical approach that carried elements of the Blue and Brown histories in them. This happened especially in academic settings with the words "whores" and "niggers" coming up actively during instruction. With the lack of discussion and context, a pre-teaching process caused the intent of instruction to produce the wrong impact.

Pre-teaching pedagogy training

Preparation toward discussion and context

Harmful stereotypes were being reinforced. Discriminatory ideologies were incubated in the classroom and impacted everyone, including non-Blue and non-Brown individuals. These individuals were conditioned to think of themselves as superior to the Blues and Browns. On the other hand, the Blue and Brown students were taught to feel and think less of themselves compared to other ethnic groups. "Although we recognize the dangers of promoting such a dynamic, the power of subconscious conditioning can overcome reason during passive states of the brain, as Dr. Haomay notes."

The classroom environment became a place for creating an ambiance of passivity while dehumanizing the Blue and Brown students. Lessons were often taught without discussion or context; the young minds of the Blue and Brown students were being conditioned into accepting the belief of their own mental inferiority. They experienced a haunting sense of isolation and were made to feel that everyone in the classroom was judging them.

A Blue receiving the shameful "spotlight" gauge

A Brown experiencing psychological judgment

With every mention of the words "whore" and "nigger," Blue and Brown students receded within the classroom and lost any sense of school as a safe and nurturing space. Any trust in their peers, teachers, and the institution was irreparably degraded. The self-worth of the unprotected Blue and Brown children eroded with every school day.

Eroded trust and safety experienced by a Blue

Eroded trust and safety experienced by a Brown

In the field of neuroscience, in which Gnalolim is well trained, experts have explained how, when our brain is clouded with emotions, it fails to function, especially when it comes to academic achievement. As a result, Blue and Brown students suffered when their ability to think critically in the classroom was compromised.

A Brown experiencing school difficulty

A Blue experiencing school difficulty

Cognitive psychologists explained that in adolescence, metacognitive states are heightened. Therefore, the emotional trauma these young people face over how others view and think of them is privileged over how they view or think about themselves. These doubts over ethnic equity are encouraged as early as the middle school years. Blue and Brown students experience derogatory microaggressions in society, and these assaults, combined with the daunting impact of discriminatory pedagogical approaches, cause these students to underperform.

Blue experiencing derogatory microaggression

Brown experiencing derogatory microaggression

Finally, the community lacks civil accountability. There is no community civility commissioner established to arbitrate matters of discriminatory practices in the community. Where do marginalized individuals, viewed as the bottom rung of their society, go when faced with incidents of sexual harassment for the Blues or ethnicity-based discrimination for the Browns? Policy initiatives must be crafted with clear guidelines, and protocols must prevent abuse and maintain effectiveness.

Brown being antagonized

Blue being antagonized

Chapter 4

Proposed Solutions from a Dispassionate-objective lens

Dr. Siramad is a policymaker and an expert in creating collaborative solutions in leadership crises. Dr. Siramad had mobilized individuals from the society and solicited their input. The collective work done by the group provided solution-oriented suggestions to solve the underlying crises in Kiaralot and Donekiaratall. They employed a qualitative and quantitative approach and generated two lists, the "opinion entry" and the "topic category catalog." The "opinion entry" was simply the summary of the suggested information received from all individuals willing to lend their voices, together with those of expert opinions in the field. The "topic-category catalog" was then generated for each proposed solution, incorporating all inputs, including the voices of the silent, dominant, minority, and majority groups. These voices received equal weight, followed by the pros and cons for each item on the "opinion entry." The process of generating the pros and cons created a template for defining the specified problem. Although everyone can have an opinion, realistically, not all ideas can lead to a solution. However, the process provided a consensus that included elements of suggested views from the diverse inputs provided. This seemingly laborious process was essential demonstrating transparency and promoted equitable solutions. The final step now was for the societies to implement the selected keys.

In both Kiaralot and Donekiaratall long, arduous debates were held year after year. At first, some people in Kiaralot didn't understand the issue under discussion; they thought the discussion process was frivolous. Some thought it might be better to eliminate any instruction of the atrocious history of the Blues and Browns altogether, in an out-of-sight, out-of-mind approach. Some argued for continuing the teaching regardless of the impact on the students, insisting that kids needed to "toughen up" to face the "reality of life" and just to "deal with it." Others suggested making every implementation optional. These discussions were intense. However, in Kiaralot, most people eventually were determined to stay focused on the singular issue at hand. The majority decided to remain committed to the cause and continued to support an all-inclusive approach to the suggested solutions.

Two key factors made the eventual dialogue healthy and productive. First, the people of Kiaralot had a civil engagement with one another in good faith. Second, all parties focused on a utilitarian approach and stayed on point in seeking equitable solutions to the stated problem. The process allowed for value integration;

hence, the choice of public values transcended personal biases, which did not come to the forefront during the decision-making process.

Results in Kiaralot

The defined problem facing the Blues and Browns was the biased pedagogical approach leading to the enforcement of harmful stereotypes and the lack of ethnic diversity integration in the school curricula.

In following the decision-making processes to create collaborative solutions, the people of Kiaralot and Donekiaratall came up with the following solutions for implementation:

1) In Kiaralot, sexual harassment education and training, and in Donekiaratall, ethnic-based discrimination education and training will have the core tenets of information, instruction, understanding, and correction.

2) In Kiaralot, the word "whores," will be referred to as the "W-word." In Donekiaratall, the word "nigger" will be referred to as the "N-word."

3) The sensitive curricular content assigned to the different grades or classes must be age-appropriate and be screened for its cognitive psychological impact on students. This process will be used to determine the design for the pedagogical training approach.

4) Alongside teaching the history of the horrific, barbaric, and inhumane acts committed against the enslaved Blues and Browns, the positive attributes of the Blues and Browns and their contributions to Kiaralot and Donekiaratall must be highlighted, celebrated, and integrated into society.

5) A deliberate attempt should be made to increase diversity in the representation of the varied ethnic groups represented in the community, including the Blues in the land of Kiaralot and the Browns in the land of Donekiaratall. This is to involve textbooks, fiction, children's games, TV shows, and the like.

The Kiaralot took these solutions onboard and implemented them judiciously. They brought about a holistic, equitable education in all their schools. The Kiaralot created civility training sessions in their communities and workforces. For the past several years, society has thrived, and Kiaralot has been considered one of the best places in the world to live.

People in Kiaralot, including the Blues, say that living happily ever after in co-existence with one another is not a dream for them but a reality.

The Kiaralots solution-oriented discussions

Value Integration – A good deal

Results in Donekiaratall

In Donekiaratall, however, the implementation of these proposed solutions was rejected. The carefully orchestrated approach in maintaining the goal of equity for all did not receive national acceptance. Other strategies were employed, but they lacked a thoughtful and thorough process. The isolation of efforts created confirmation biases in ideas; compromises left both parties feeling dissatisfied by the tactics used to create dominating ideologies. These approaches used by the people of Donekiaratall did not lend themselves to value integration for a solution-oriented focus. Instead, failed problem-solving led to the creation of more problems.

The Blues have joined the Browns for centuries to resist dehumanizing stereotypes that set one ethnic group against another. More importantly, they have bonded to eliminate social inequities toward marginalized ethnic groups. The movement is a call to all ethnic groups of our human race to join a multiethnic coalition and to work against discriminatory ideologies together.

Our mother, Dlyl, continues to dedicate herself to the education, support, and advocacy for equity that will promote the expression of authentic ethnicity, uphold ethnic identity, and challenge social norms that perpetuate hate and self-hate.

Bringing it close to home

In our human societies, our shared history has within it untold atrocities exercised against targeted groups. We must realize that the brain mechanisms underlying these social-behavioral outputs are not extinct. The lingering residues continue to show as discriminatory tendencies. The psychological disease caused by prolonged dehumanization and harmful stereotypes has led to trauma on the impacted. Treatment options should undoubtedly begin with preventative measures. Firstly, the removal of the causative agents of discrimination producing this societal, psychological disease is imperative. The postface in this book throws some light on understanding the neural basis underlying facial and skin tone recognition and its connection to the brain's fear centers, leading to discriminatory and hateful behaviors.

Thank you for reading this story; however, join the call to complete the story - what you do or do not do will determine our end to be one of hope-realized **(as** in Kiaralot – "Care-alot") or hope-deferred (as in Donekiaratall – "Don't-care-at-all").

Postface

POSTFACE

A call to embrace a racially diverse and inclusive curriculum: Shifting the paradigm to provide racial-ethnic equity by understanding a simplified summary of neuro – socio dynamics associated with classical conditioning

"Dark skin toned folks carrying the social attributes of blackness are perceived guilty until proven innocent, while light skin toned folks carrying the social attributes of whiteness are perceived innocent until proven guilty."

Abstract

Observations surrounding biases, discrimination, and hate weaved in our social fabric have received diverse perspectives. – philosophically, psychologically, sociologically, and to some extent, neurologically. In recent times, there has been an increased social awareness and ethical implications regarding the call for culturally responsive curricular in our schools and the society as a whole. Judicious work is underway to provide rich assessment tools that could help combat discriminatory and biased practices. One such tool is the call to use CR-SE (culturally responsive-student education), where students use their own identity to get an education. Studies show that students learning with CR-SE obtain improved self-esteem, have better grades, and graduate more often (Villegas, 1991; Bennett, 2008). However, combating racial inequity cannot be about awareness alone but by understanding the neuronal mechanisms underlying the occurrences expressed in inequitable social behaviors and the factors triggering these mechanisms. This understanding will provide the knowledge to drive the concerted effort needed to exert purposeful changes toward racial equity practices in our schools and communities. This paper reviews part of the neuronal mechanism underlying the expression of social behaviors, which can extrapolate to the characterized social behaviors expressed in colorism and racism.

Conceptual Framework

Recognizing the root problem – harmful ideologies and negative stereotypes perpetuate prejudices (Allport et al., 1954), causing inequities. Destructive ideologies continue to be mentally reinforced and propagated by the process of classical conditioning. Classical conditioning is a learning process where an unconditioned stimulus that triggers an unconditioned response leading to a behavioral output becomes associated with another "orchestrated" neuronal input (the conditioned stimulus) that triggers a conditioned response producing the same behavioral output as the unconditioned response (Davies et al., 1982; Eelen, 2018). In other words, negative stereotypes by association to race discriminatory ideologies impact neuronal perceptions creating prejudices and unconscious biases. - "Dark skin-toned folks by association to "black" carry the social attributes of blackness - perceived guilty until proven innocent. On the contrary, light skin-toned folks by association to "white" carry the social attributes of whiteness - perceived innocent until proven guilty."

Introduction

Humans are complex species ascribing to several dimensions-S.N.I.C.S: the supernatural (spiritual), the natural (physical), intuitiveness (mind), the consciousness (soul), the social (secular) (Legare et al., 2012; Oman, 2014). In focusing solely on the natural and social sciences, the question of interest explores the possible impact of external factors impacting neuronal mechanisms underlying the expression of social behaviors characterized by colorism (Dixon and Telles, 2017) and racism (Memmi, 2000; Harris, 2008; Miles, 2004). Biologists - natural scientists studying the natural or physical aspects of life, attribute the primary control of our human biological systems to the intricate work of the nervous and endocrine systems (Sherwood, 2015). In focusing on the nervous system, there are several brain areas involved in social behaviors. However, exploring five such regions to understand the mechanisms underlying the neuronal basis of racial-ethnic inequities. These areas include the frontal cortex; fusiform nuclei areas; amygdala nuclei areas; insula cortex; and anterior cingulate gyrus (Sapolsky, 2017).

Classical Conditioning

Concept of <u>Whiteness</u>

Light Pure Clean
Bright Acceptable
Joy Life
Harmless Safe
Innocent Angelic Brightness
Transparent Honorable

Concept of <u>Blackness</u>

Dark Fifthly Dirty
Gloomy Rejected
Sad Death
Dangerous Threatening
Guilty Devilish Darkness
Skirmish Dishonest

Figure 1: Illustration of classical conditioning: Photo credits, courtesy, and adoption: Asia Milia Ware. Diminishing Representation Efforts. 2020; Dr. Damaris-Lois Y Lang. Classical conditioning concepts. 2021

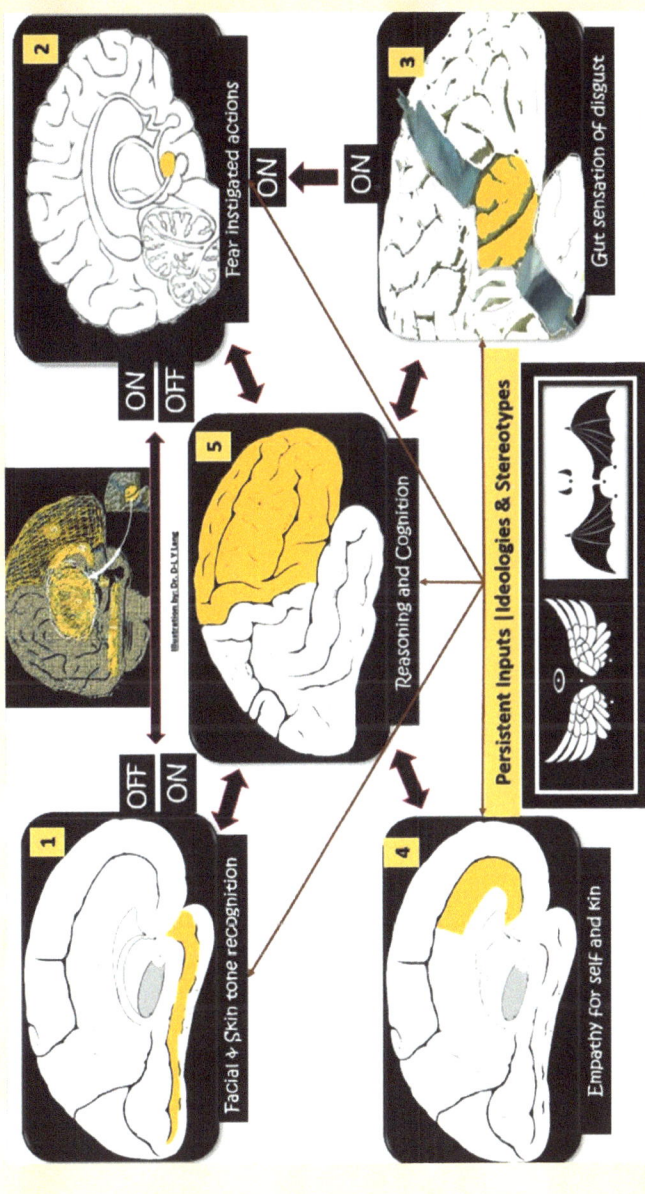

Figure 2: Illustration of the neuronal regions involved in the mechanisms underlying behaviors indicative of racial inequity influenced by external inputs: Photo credit: Individual Brain map credit: Henry Gray (1825-1861). Anatomy of the Human Body. 1918; Illustration: Dr. Damaris-Lois Y Lang. Brain Connection Illustration. 2021. (Brain Regions: [1] the fusiform nuclei areas; [2] the amygdala nuclei areas; [3] the insula cortex; [4] the anterior cingulate gyrus; [5] the frontal cortex.

Neuro-Socio Behaviors Associated with Skin Color tones

Summary of selected neural areas implicated in behavior inequities associated with social differences

The description provided for each of the selected brain areas is a fraction of the function and roles they play in the body (refer to figure 2).

[1]   The Fusiform nuclei areas of the brain are known to play an essential role in recognizing facial forms, including the skin color tones of individuals. The learned process is from the neonate years throughout adulthood (Grill-Spector et al., 2004; Fenker., 2005; Kanwisher, N et al., 2006).

-The social, behavioral output of interest is recognizing facial and skin tone characteristics of racial-ethnic groups.

[2]   The amygdala nuclei areas of the brain are partly involved in instigating behavioral output related to fear, ranging from a cautionary stance to very aggressive forms (Adolphs et al., 1995; Choe et al., 2015. Sapolsky, 2017).

- The social, behavioral output of interest is that of fear provoked caution or hostility against the perceived threat towards blackness, a classical-conditioned attribution.

[3]   The insula cortex perceives disgust to rancid gustatory (taste) input and actions perceived as unethical or immoral. The neuronal process can cause the stimulation of the viscera of the gut and provide the physical sensation of "feeling sick in the gut" (Wicker et al., 2003; Sprengelmeyer, 2007' Uddin et al., 2017; Sapolsky, 2017).

- The social, behavioral output of interest is the disgust one experiences against another by the individual's subjective notion of a perceived state, being, or action, deemed unacceptable, unethical, or immoral.

[4]   The anterior cingulate gyrus is involved in conflict error detection and the emotional reaction to pain (Gu et al., 2010; Apps et al., 2016; Sapolsky, 2017).

-The social, behavioral output of interest is the choice, without added context, between expressing empathy towards varied racial-ethnic groups.

[5]   The frontal cortex of our brain is the area involved in reasoning, assessing, thinking, abstract perceptions, and many other higher cognitive functions to aid in the final decision-making process in our behavioral outputs (Duncan and Owen, 2000; Mendez et al., 2005).

-The social, behavioral output of interest is the final judgment in the decision-making processes.

Connecting the Neuro-Socio Dynamics of Classical Conditioned Behaviors related to Skin Color tones:

Brain plasticity may continue throughout life (Kolb, 2013); however, the maturation of the frontal cortex occurs relatively late, around 25 years (Johnson et al., 2009). Late maturation of the frontal cortex may be necessary to allow for more deliberate and desirable decision-making determination processes towards the display of behavioral output (Sapolsky, 2017). Like many other brain areas, the frontal cortex relies on external and internal inputs, including inputs from different brain areas, to execute an executive function (Andrés, 2003). External inputs from most societies have provided the overall abstract representation of black versus white (refer to figure 1) followed by enforced neuronal association of color themes observed in Stroop test analysis (Stroop, 1935), creating skin color tone dichotomy into black and white. Skin tones categorization has birthed the harmful ideology of whiteness, by association to white -a desirable trait over blackness, by association to black -an undesirable trait. There is an inequitable judgment that results from the concept of embracing whiteness as good while eschewing blackness as bad (Fishkin, 1995; Guess, 2006). As such birthing the global social awareness of biases embedded in the social characterizations – colorism and racism (Hochschild and Weaver, 2007; Hunter, 2007; Uzogara et al., 2014). Dark skin-toned individuals carry the social attributes of blackness (undesirable abstract association), often perceived guilty until proven innocent. Alternatively, light-skinned folks take the social qualities of whiteness (a desirable abstract association) (Spencer, 1984) are perceived innocent until proven guilty. This social state of colorism and racial inequities may result in associating dark-skin-toned individuals with the abstract negative concept of black compared to white. This classically conditioned mindset can shape the brain to exhibit skewed perceptions based on an individual's skin tone, leading to unfair and inequitable treatment in societal race-related behaviors. Darker skin-toned folks are often deemed inferior globally, as shown in the social constructs of colorism and racism (Amir et al., 2005).

Societal systems provide a narrower positive representation of dark-skin-toned individuals. The few showcased dark-skin-toned individuals often are portrayed with negative stereotypes (Grafman and Hollnagel, 1996). Harmful ideologies and negative stereotypes associated with darker skin-toned individuals cause the activation of the insula cortex to provide the perception of disgust (Wicker et al., 2003; Sprengelmeyer, 2007; Sapolsky, 2017) towards perceived notions an individual carries as a compass against dark skin-toned individuals (Spencer, 1984). For instance, such concepts can include an imposed judgment such as the subconscious mindset of the inconceivable placement of dark-skin-toned individuals deemed as inferior over lighter-skin-toned individuals in positions of authority (Bell, 1988). Studies show that such perceived unethical notions can produce a physical gut sensation of disgust against the deemed perpetrator by sheer mentally imposed superiority (Sapolsky, 2017). Also, the normalization of white racial identity serving as the standard by which all other groups compare causes the anterior cingulate gyrus to extend a sense of empathy (Lavin et al., 2013) towards whiteness over blackness (Blair et al., 2004). Another neuronal mechanism of great importance is the fusiform–amygdala interplay. Facial and skin-toned recognition is a learned behavior that starts from the neonate years throughout adulthood (Loffler et al., 2005). Neuronal studies show that facial recognition difficulties such as those of different ethnicities (race) correspond to decreased activation in the brain's fusiform area while simultaneously increasing the amygdala-the fear centers (Kanwisher and Yovel, 2006). Preventing this instinctive interplay between the decreased-fusiform and increased-amygdala activation impacting the underrepresented in a heterogeneous society will require increased acquainting of unfamiliar ethnic groups across the varied ethnicities. By classical conditioning, when there is a perceived unpleasant stimulus from an individual, the activation of the amygdala can occur. Amygdala activation serves as an intuitive way to alert the body to act momentarily to provide protection and self-survival (Choe et al., 2015). The activated amygdala hostility provoked behavior (Adolphs et al., 1995; Choe et al., 2015) may heighten towards darker skin-toned individuals compared to light skin-toned individuals. One of the neuronal mechanisms that may delay an amygdala provoked hostile behavior is the frontal cortex's agility to assess the situation more fairly (Mendez et al., 2005) and rationally (Brower et al., 2001). There is a lack of positive representation in social outlets, entertainment (Smith, I. ed. Neill and Schalkwyk 2016), media (Duke, 2012; Jha, 2015), and curriculum related to dark-skin-toned individuals (Spencer, 1984; Hochschild and Weaver, 2007). Reducing amygdala activation based on unfamiliarity and negative stereotypes will require a mental shift to familiarity coupled with a more positive association towards dark-skin-toned individuals. In situations of emotional reaction related to pain in conflict resolution scenarios, the criminalization of blackness is the default creating the extension of harsher judgment against dark-skin-toned individuals compared to light-skin-toned individuals (Uzogara et al., 2014). Less lenient measures towards dark skin tone offenders are much higher than for light skin toned folks (Gallagher and Poletti, 1998; Blair et al., 2004).

A Solution-Oriented Direction

Impact on Education:

Darker skin-toned individuals often face a stereotype threat-a predicament in society that adds to school difficulty (Rosenberg, 1965; Spencer, 1994). Studies have shown that the brain clouded with emotions does not perform rationally (Eisenberger et al., 2003), including academic achievement, especially in adolescents who exhibit massive changes in cognitive and metacognitive states (Johnson et al., 2009). Most curricular literature referred to as "the classics" lacks racial diversity and is dominated by light-skin-toned characters (McKinley, 2010). In the USA, for instance, most educators within the school systems are predominantly light-skin-toned individuals (Gay and Howard, 2000; Bates and Glick, 2013). Bringing ethnic diversity in educational settings is necessary to facilitate a more rigorous inspirational engagement vital to students' academic successes as students see and identify themselves in their learning materials and teachers (Rosenberg, 1965; Brown, 1998; Gay and Howard, 2000; Hunter, 2007). The practical integration of rich, in-depth positive representation of the socially disadvantaged is essential in combating negative stereotypes.

The affirmative action approach:

The next is to work collectively as one human race and combat ideologies perpetuating colorism and racial inequities. A simple first step is being intentional in acquainting ourselves and our kids with other ethnic groups, actively normalizing the diversity of all of our unique individuality as beauty radiating under the sun. A good amount of most of our waking time is spent in places of work or for our kids, schools. It is imperative to make an effort to increase racial diversity in these institutions (Coffey and Farinde-Wu, 2016). However, being that the underrepresented racial groups are also the minority in number will require a robust approach in recruitment strategies (Allen, 1992, Coffey and Farinde-Wu,

2016). The lack of ethnic-racial responsive educational endeavors in our schools and society has an enormous negative impact on the brain (Kumaran et al., 2016), impacting social behaviors. The calculation presented (refer to Table 1) is accurate for any person, whether in the minority or the majority, assuming that there are no biases towards a specific racial/ethnic group. The quest for public value integration related to racial equity in this simple math calculation reveals the slim chances of securing job positions for the underrepresented minority by sheer probability. Analysis shows that not seeking out processes to ascertain affirmative action (Gamson and Modigliani, 1994; Kellough, 2006) procedures and protocols towards public value equitable integration in schools and communities will leave us right where we are- a society perpetually battling racial inequity.

Table 1: Simple Calculation with an Assumption of a System Upholding Racial Equity

RACIALLY UNDERREPRESENTED PROFESSIONAL FIELD

Calculation for a Hypothetical Scenarios		Summary
Non-Persons of Color	Persons of Color	
80 (Individuals) = 80%	20 (individuals) = 20%	The calculation presented is true for any one person, whether in the minority or the majority. However, in the quest for public value integration related to racial equity, this simple math calculation reveals, by sheer probability, the slim chances of securing the underrepresented for a position. Without considering pre-conceived and biased racial attributes, the analysis reveals that not seeking out processes to ascertain affirmative action procedures and protocols towards public value equitable integration in schools and communities will leave us right where we are-a racial inequity society.
One out of two are ideally suited for vacant positions (50%)		
40 (Individuals)	10 (Individuals)	
Individuals equally distributed across 5 vacancies in separate/same Regions/Districts		
40/5 = 8 (Individuals)	10/5 = 2 (Individuals)	
	% of Black POC's?	
	0 - 2 (individuals)	

Hiring the underrepresented will require an intentional seeking out-an incorporated affirmative action rubric

Conclusion

The shared spaces of our public education and societal endeavors in our schools and communities must hold an equitable integration of the varying skin tones exhibited in our human race. Unconscious biases happen to the best of us, within cultures (such as colorism) and across cultures (such as racism). Recognize that harmful ideologies and negative stereotypes serve as external inputs in stimulating our brain circuitry, which then feeds into our minds and produces our varied mindsets, producing inequitable behaviors. The way forward is not about blame but rather understanding. Negate harmful ideologies and negative stereotypes against one another. Introduce positive input into our thought processes utilizing the higher centers in the cognitive areas of the brain to feed into the neuronal circuitry, which then shapes the mind and, in turn, our mindsets, ultimately influencing an equitable behavioral output.

References

1) Allen, W. (1992). The color of success: African-American college student outcomes at predominantly White and historically Black public colleges and universities. Harvard Educational Review, 62(1), 26-45.

2) Allport, G.W., Clark, K., & Pettigrew, T. (1954). The nature of prejudice.

3) Amir, N., Klumpp, H., Elias, J., Bedwell, J. S., Yanasak, N., & Miller, L. S. (2005). Increased activation of the anterior cingulate cortex during processing of disgust faces in individuals with social phobia. Biological psychiatry, 57(9), 975-981.

4) Andrés, P. (2003). Frontal cortex as the central executive of working memory: time to revise our view. Cortex, 39(4-5), 871-895.

5) Apps, M. A., Rushworth, M. F., & Chang, S. W. (2016). The anterior cingulate gyrus and social cognition: tracking the motivation of others. Neuron, 90(4), 692-707.

6) Adolphs, R., Tranel, D., Damasio, H., Damasio, A.R. (1995). Fear and the human amygdala. The Journal of Neuroscience, 15, 5879–5892.

7) Bates, L. A., & Glick, J. E. (2013). Does it matter if teachers and schools match the student? Racial and ethnic disparities in problem behaviors. Social science research, 42(5), 1180-1190.

8) Bell, D. (1988). White superiority in America: Its legal legacy, its economic costs. Villanova Law Review, 33, 767.

9) Brown, KT. (1998). Skin tone bias and African-American well-being: A dual influence model approach. University of Michigan, Ann Arbor, Michigan, PhD dissertation (AAT 9909861).

10) Blair, I.V., Judd, C.M., & Chapleau, K.M. (2004). The influence of Afrocentric facial features in criminal sentencing. Psychological Science,15, 674–679.

11) Brower, M. C., & Price, B. H. (2001). Neuropsychiatry of frontal lobe dysfunction in violent and criminal behaviour: a critical review. Journal of Neurology, Neurosurgery & Psychiatry, 71(6), 720-726.

12) Choe, D. E., Shaw, D. S., & Forbes, E. E. (2015). Maladaptive social information processing in childhood predicts young men's atypical amygdala reactivity to threat. Journal of Child Psychology and Psychiatry, 56(5), 549-557.

13) Coffey, H., & Farinde-Wu, A. (2016). Navigating the journey to culturally responsive teaching: Lessons from the success and struggles of one first-year, Black female teacher of Black students in an urban school. Teaching and Teacher Education, 60, 24-33.

14) Cummings, J.L. (1993). Frontal-subcortical circuits and human behavior. Archives of Neurology, 50, 873–880.

15) Davies, P., Davies, G. L., & Bennett, S. (1982). An effective paradigm for conditioning visual perception in human subjects. Perception, 11(6), 663-669.

16) Dimitrov, M., Grafman, J., & Hollnagel, C. (1996). The effects of frontal lobe damage on everyday problem solving. Cortex, 32, 357–366.

17) Dixon, A. R., & Telles, E. E. (2017). Skin color and colorism: Global research, concepts, and measurement. Annual Review of Sociology, 43, 405-424.

18) Duke, A. (2012). Acura apologizes for seeking 'not too dark' actor. CNN. Apr 19, 2012, Retrieved from http://www.cnn.com/2012/04/18/showbiz/acura-ad-controversy/index.html.

19) Duncan, J., & Owen, A.M. (2000). Common regions of the human frontal lobe recruited by diverse cognitive demands. Trends Neuroscience, 23, 475–483.

20) Eelen, P. (2018). Classical Conditioning: Classical Yet Modern. Psychologica Belgica, 58(1), 196–211.

21) Eisenberger, NI., Lieberman, MD, & Williams, KD. (2003). Does rejection hurt? An fMRI study of social exclusion. Science, 302, 290-292.

22) Fenker, D. B., Schott, B. H., Richardson Klavehn, A., Heinze, H. J., & Düzel, E. (2005). Recapitulating emotional context: activity of

amygdala, hippocampus and fusiform cortex during recollection and familiarity. European Journal of Neuroscience, 21(7), 1993-1999.

23) Fishkin, S. F. (1995). Interrogating" whiteness," complicating" blackness": Remapping American culture. American Quarterly, 47(3), 428-466.

24) Gallagher, P., & Poletti, P. (1998). Sentencing disparity and the ethnicity of juvenile offenders (No. 17). Sydney: Judicial Commission of New South Wales.

25) Gamson, W. A., & Modigliani, A. (1994). The changing culture of affirmative action. Equal employment opportunity: labor market discrimination and public policy, 3, 373-394.

26) Gay, G., & Howard, T. C. (2000). Multicultural teacher education for the 21st century. The teacher educator, 36(1), 1-16.

27) Grill-Spector, K., Knouf, N., & Kanwisher, N. (2004). The fusiform face area subserves face perception, not generic within-category identification. Nature neuroscience, 7(5), 555-562.

28) Gu, X., Liu, X., Guise, K. G., Naidich, T. P., Hof, P. R., & Fan, J. (2010). Functional dissociation of the frontoinsular and anterior cingulate cortices in empathy for pain. Journal of Neuroscience, 30(10), 3739-3744.

29) Guess, T. J. (2006). The social construction of whiteness: Racism by intent, racism by consequence. Critical Sociology, 32(4), 649-673.

30) Harris, A. P. (2008). From color line to color chart: Racism and colorism in the new century. Berkeley J. Afr.-Am. L. & Pol'y, 10, 52.

31) Hochschild, J.L., & Weaver, V. (2007). The skin color paradox and the American racial order. Social Forces, 86, 643–670.

32) Holtzman J. (1973) Color caste changes among Black college students. Journal of Black Studies, 4, 92–101.

33) Hunter, M. (2007). The persistent problem of colorism: Skin tone, status, and inequality. Sociology compass, 1(1), 237-254.

34) Jha, M. (2015). The Global Beauty Industry: Colorism, Racism, and the National Body (1st ed.). Routledge.

35) Johnson, S. B., Blum, R. W., & Giedd, J. N. (2009). Adolescent maturity and the brain: the promise and pitfalls of neuroscience research in adolescent health policy. Journal of Adolescent Health, 45(3), 216-221.

36) Kolb, B. (2013). Brain plasticity and behavior. Psychology Press.

37) Kumaran, D., Banino A., Blundell C., Hassabis D., & Dayan P. (2016). Computations Underlying Social Hierarchy Learning: Distinct

Neural Mechanisms for Updating and Representing Self-Relevant Information, Neuron, 92, 1135-1147.

38) Kanwisher, N., & Yovel, G. (2006). The fusiform face area: a cortical region specialized for the perception of faces. Philosophical Transactions of the Royal Society B: Biological Sciences, 361(1476), 2109-2128.

39) Kellough, J. E. (2006). Understanding affirmative action Georgetown University Press, Washington, DC, 191.

40) Lavin, C., Melis, C., Mikulan, E. P., Gelormini, C., Huepe, D., & Ibañez, A. (2013). The anterior cingulate cortex: an integrative hub for human socially-driven interactions. Frontiers in neuroscience, 7, 64.

41) Legare, C. H., Evans, E. M., Rosengren, K. S., & Harris, P. L. (2012). The coexistence of natural and supernatural explanations across cultures and development. Child development, 83(3), 779-793.

42) Loffler, G., Yourganov, G., Wilkinson, F., & Wilson, H. R. (2005). fMRI evidence for the neural representation of faces. Nature neuroscience, 8(10), 1386-1391.

43) McKinley, J. (2010). Raising black students' achievement through culturally responsive teaching. ASCD.

44) Memmi, A. (2000). Racism. University of Minnesota Press.

45) Mendez, M. F., Anderson, E., & Shapira, J. S. (2005). An investigation of moral judgement in frontotemporal dementia. Cognitive and behavioral neurology, 18(4), 193-197.

46) Miles, R. (2004). Racism. Routledge.

47) Oman, J. (2014). The Natural and the Supernatural. Cambridge University Press.

48) Rosenberg, M. (1965). Society and the adolescent self-image. Princeton, N.J: Princeton University Press

49) Sapolsky, R.M. (2017). Behave: The biology of humans at our best and worst. Penguin.

50) Sherwood, L. (2015). Human physiology: from cells to systems. Cengage learning.

51) Smith, I., Edited by Neill, M., & Schalkwyk, D. (2016). Seeing Blackness. In The Oxford Handbook of Shakespearean Tragedy.

52) Spencer, M.B. (1984). Black children's race awareness, racial attitudes and self-concept: A reinterpretation. Journal of Child Psychology and Psychiatry, 25, 433–441.

53) Sprengelmeyer, R. (2007). The neurology of disgust. Brain, 130(7), 1715-1717.

54) Uddin, L.Q., Nomi, J.S., Hébert-Seropian, B., Ghaziri, J., & Boucher, O. (2017). Structure and Function of the Human Insula. Journal of Clinical Neurophysiology, 34(4), 300–306.

55) Stroop, J. R. (1935). Studies of interference in serial verbal reactions. Journal of Experimental Psychology, 18(6), 643–662.

56) Uzogara, E.E., Lee, H., Abdou, C.M., & Jackson, J.S. (2014). A comparison of skin tone discrimination among African American men: 1995 and 2003. Psychology of men & masculinity, 15(2), 201–212.

57) Wicker, B., Keysers, C., Plailly, J., Royet, J. P., Gallese, V., & Rizzolatti, G. (2003). Both of us disgusted in My insula: the common neural basis of seeing and feeling disgust. Neuron, 40(3), 655-664.